FOCUS ON THE FAMILY PRESENTS

THE IMAGINATION STATION®

Light in the Lions' Den

BOOK 19

MARIANNE HERING
ILLUSTRATIONS BY DAVID HOHN

TYNDALE

FOCUS ON THE FAMILY • ADVENTURES IN ODYSSEY®
TYNDALE HOUSE PUBLISHERS, INC. • CAROL STREAM, ILLINOIS

To Liz Duckworth

Contents

Prologue   1

1   The Imagination Station   5
2   The Statue   10
3   In the Desert   17
4   The Hanging Gardens   23
5   The Gates of Babylon   37
6   The Temple of Adad   46
7   Inside the Palace   56
8   The Advisers' Plan   67
9   Two Kings   78
10 Daniel   86
11 The New Law   92
12 King Darius's Regret   100
13 The Open Window   108
14 The Arrest   113
15 The Angel   122
16 The Imagination Station Returns   133
    Secret Word Puzzle   137

Prologue

At Whit's End, a lightning storm zapped the Imagination Station's computer. Then the Imagination Station began to do strange things. It took the cousins to the wrong adventures. The machine also gave the wrong gifts.

Mr. Whittaker was gone. Eugene was in charge of the workshop. He and Beth found an older version of the Imagination Station. It looked like a car. It had a special feature called *lockdown mode.* The cousins began using this machine for their adventures.

Eugene wanted to keep the cousins safe. He went with Patrick on an adventure to protect him. But the Imagination Station separated him from Patrick. Eugene was lost in history.

In book 18, *Trouble on the Orphan Train,* the cousins searched for Eugene. And Eugene had indeed entered their adventure in 1874. But a detective named Mr. Pinkerton thought Eugene was a criminal.

Mr. Pinkerton locked Eugene in jail. He took away the computer Eugene needed to help them get home.

Later the detective arrested the cousins, too. He brought Patrick and Beth to Eugene's jail cell.

Suddenly the car-like Imagination Station appeared.

Here's what happened next . . .

Patrick and Beth rushed into the cell.

"Hurry," Patrick said. "Get in the

machine. What are you waiting for, Eugene?"

Patrick stared at his friend. Eugene looked glum.

"Your plan has a flaw," Eugene said. "There are only two seats in this machine."

"So one of us has to stay behind," Beth said. It was a fact. Not a question.

Patrick heard a click. He turned.

Mr. Pinkerton had locked the cell.

The Imagination Station

Mr. Pinkerton said, "You will *all* stay behind bars. At least till I talk to the Little Rock judge. I need to ask him what to do with children. I've never arrested kids before."

Mr. Pinkerton put the key in his pocket. He tipped his hat with a nod. Then the detective walked away from the jail cell. He headed up the stairs.

Beth gasped. She turned toward Eugene. "What should we do?" she asked.

Eugene stood up straight. He took a deep breath.

"I'll take the risk and go," Eugene said. "I'm fairly certain I can get back to Whit's End."

"What if you can't?" Patrick asked. "Beth and I will rot in jail if it doesn't work."

Just then Patrick heard loud footsteps coming from the stairwell.

Eugene moved toward the cell's bars. "Mr. Pinkerton is coming back!" he said.

A popping sound came from the corner of the cell. Patrick and Beth turned to look.

The Imagination Station was fading in and out.

Just then Mr. Pinkerton appeared. "I forgot to ask about that 'computer' you have," he said. "It looks like a typewriter. But I opened it, and it doesn't have any ink inside."

Eugene groaned. "You opened it," he said. "With what?"

"A crowbar," the detective said.

Patrick quickly moved to Beth. He grabbed her wrist and pulled her toward the Imagination Station. "We have to get out of here now. Or the machine might disappear."

"Wait!" Beth said. "What about Eugene?"

"We'll come back for him," Patrick whispered. "He'll be okay. It's

not as if Mr. Pinkerton will throw him to the lions."

The cousins got into the car-like Imagination Station. They shut the doors and fastened their seat belts.

Patrick grabbed the black knob on the dashboard. A sharp pain shot up his hand to his elbow. He let the knob go. "Ouch!" he said. "It shocked me!"

He looked at Beth. Wisps of her dark-brown hair were sticking straight up.

"There's a lot of static electricity inside the car," Beth said. She reached over and took Patrick's hand. "I don't want to get separated again."

Patrick nodded. Then he glanced out the windshield. Eugene and Mr. Pinkerton were still talking. Patrick heard Mr. Pinkerton say, "I have the evidence that you were part of the robbery right here in this satchel!"

Patrick yanked the black knob again. He ignored the tingles that shocked him.

He heard an electric buzz as the car began to spin. Sparks flew off the outside of the car.

Beth gripped Patrick's free hand tightly.

The windshield filled with bright, swirling colors. Patrick felt as if they were being sucked into a whirlpool. The temperature dropped, and a chill seeped into his bones.

Suddenly everything went black.

The Statue

The Imagination Station stopped moving.

Beth tried looking out the windshield. She saw only swirling rainbow colors.

Beth squeezed Patrick's hand. He squeezed hers back. *At least Patrick and I are still together*, she thought.

A pang of guilt stabbed her heart. Her friend Eugene was alone in jail. She hadn't even said good-bye.

Then Beth noticed a weird feeling on her

skin. She felt tingling on her back and legs. She wanted out of the machine.

Beth let go of Patrick's hand and pulled on the door handle. It wouldn't budge.

"We're in lockdown mode," Patrick whispered. "We can't get out. It's not safe."

Suddenly the windshield cleared. The car was on the ground in a sandy plain. A few palm trees were clumped together here and there. Small rock piles were nearby.

In the far distance was a city. A tall blue-and-tan wall surrounded it.

A crowd of people stood a few hundred feet away. They were dressed in brightly colored clothes. The car rolled toward them. They couldn't see the Imagination Station.

The men in the crowd wore hats covered in cloth. The hats were shaped like upside-down sand buckets.

The women's clothes had many layers of tunics and scarves. Their headdresses were decorated with jewels and fringe.

The car stopped in front of a giant statue. The statue stood on a tall platform.

Patrick craned his neck to look up at the statue. "Wow," he said, "it's like a gold Statue of Liberty."

"No, it's not," Beth said. "The Statue of Liberty is a woman. This statue is a man. Don't you see his funny-looking beard?"

"I didn't say it's *exactly* like the Statue of Liberty," Patrick said. "I meant it's gigantic."

Just then, a loud horn sounded. The noise came from the speakers in the Imagination Station's ceiling.

Beth watched as the people in the crowd approached the statue. They knelt in

front of it and bowed low. Their foreheads touched the sand.

Next a voice came from the speakers. It said, "King Nebuchadnezzar of Babylon made a statue of himself. The king wanted everyone to worship him. The people had to bow to the statue whenever a horn blasted. If they did not, guards would throw them into a molten-hot furnace."

Suddenly, bright flashes of orange, red, and white light filled the windshield. The car began to feel hot. The light hurt Beth's eyes.

"It's fire!" Beth shouted. She lifted her forearms across her face. It helped block out the bright light.

The voice said, "Three Jewish men would not bow and worship the statue. Their names were Shadrach, Meshach, and Abednego. They believed in the one true God. King

Nebuchadnezzar got angry with them. He wanted them to die. So the king's guards threw the three men into the molten-hot furnace."

The voice fell silent.

Beth leaned toward Patrick. "I remember this from church," she whispered. "It's a Bible story."

Beth dropped her arms and squinted. She could see three men in the fiery furnace. They were wearing brightly colored robes. They also wore upside-down bucket hats.

"Look," Patrick said, "there are four men in the furnace now."

Beth squinted harder till she saw the new man. He had on a white robe, and his head was uncovered.

Beth thought the new man was handsome and strong. He looked perfectly formed. He was like a Roman statue come to life.

"The new guy is glowing even brighter than the fire," Patrick said. "Why isn't everyone burning up?"

Then the speaker said, "Men into the molten-hot furnace, molten-hot furnace, molten-hot . . ."

The windshield turned dark. The car grew cold. The tingling in Beth's legs hurt.

A bolt of lightning flashed across the windshield. Beth heard a bang of thunder. The sound rattled her ears.

Another bolt flashed.

Beth closed her eyes. She clapped her hands over her ears and waited. Minutes passed. Then the lightning storm stopped.

Beth yanked on the door again. This time it flew open. She fell out of the Imagination Station and landed facedown in the sand.

3

In the Desert

Patrick was lying on top of a large sand dune. He pushed himself up to his elbows. He noticed several small formations in the desert sand. They looked like dead tree roots.

He stood and then glanced at Beth.

His cousin had a funny look on her face. Then she stuck out her tongue. Patrick saw it was speckled with grains of sand.

Beth spit out the grit. "Yuck! I'd give anything for a drink of water right now."

Patrick looked around. The Imagination Station was gone. They were in the same area as the crowds of bowing people. Sand, rocks, and palm trees spread out before him. The morning sun was low in the sky.

The walled city of Babylon stood in the distance. But not everything was the same.

"What happened to the statue of that man?" Patrick asked. "It's gone."

Beth stood up and glanced around. Then she looked at Patrick and giggled.

"What's so funny?" Patrick asked.

"You're dressed in a bathrobe," Beth said.

Patrick looked down at his clothes. He was wearing a tan tunic with a long brown coat over it. His belt was orange.

He wiggled his toes in the sandals.

"What about you?" Patrick said. "Your outfit isn't normal either."

Beth wore a purple dress and sandals.

"So are we in Bible times?" Patrick asked.

"I'm not sure," Beth said. "These outfits look right. But we could be anywhere at any time."

Patrick said, "Maybe the Imagination Station shut down and just dropped us off. That's not the only thing wrong with it. It's been sending useless gifts."

Beth gasped. She looked up and then shouted, "Watch out!"

Patrick felt Beth's shoulder push into his ribs, hard. She moved him about two feet.

Patrick fell backward. "Hey!" he shouted. Beth landed right next to him.

Patrick heard a soft thud in the sand. He looked where they'd been standing.

"I forgot to tell you something important," Beth said. "The Imagination Station is dropping the gifts from the sky."

Several small objects fell on the sand. They landed next to the strange root-like formations. Two of the new gifts were old-fashioned cans. A strange yellow object was lying next to them.

Beth crawled over to the cans. She picked up one of them. The label was white with

red writing on it. She read the label out loud: "It says, 'Corned Beef. Made in U.S.A.'"

Beth stood and picked up the yellow object. It was made of plastic. The gadget was about the size of a small TV remote control. It had symbols and dials on it.

"It's electronic with a digital display," she said. "It looks like something Mr. Whittaker or Eugene would use."

Patrick stood and brushed the
sand off his clothes. Beth handed
him the gadget.

"It's some kind of electric
meter," Patrick said. "I wonder
why the light is flashing red.
There was no electricity during
this time period."

Patrick tossed the yellow meter in the
sand. "We don't need it. But we may need
the corned beef."

"*You* can take the canned meat," Beth
said. She bent and picked up the yellow
object. "I'll keep this. We might need it."

Beth put the gizmo into her skirt pocket.

Patrick picked up the two cans of corned
beef. Each had a small metal key attached.

The cans were too heavy to put in Patrick's
pockets. So he carried one can in each hand.

"Should we go to the city?" Beth asked.

"There's nowhere else to go," Patrick said. "And we need water."

Patrick trudged off. He put a hand up to shade his eyes. "Finding water isn't our only problem," he said. "Look."

Patrick pointed toward the city.

Two chariots were rolling quickly across the sand. A cloud of dust followed them.

"They're coming toward us," Beth said.

Patrick sighed. He dropped the cans in the sand and plopped down next to them.

"What are you doing?" Beth asked. "Shouldn't we run away?"

"There's nowhere to go," Patrick said. He motioned toward the open space. "Let the chariot drivers come get us. They're probably going to make us their slaves anyway."

The Hanging Gardens

Patrick heard a loud, deep sound. It broke the silence of the desert.

One of the chariot drivers must have blown a horn.

The chariots were close enough that Patrick could see them better. Each chariot had two wheels and one driver. A single horse pulled each chariot.

The men in the chariots wore pointed

helmets. Patrick guessed they were soldiers.

The chariots stopped only ten feet away from the cousins. The horses were breathing heavily. One of the animals stomped a front hoof.

The two soldiers stayed inside their chariots. One of the men raised a horn to his lips. He blew into it. Three loud blasts sounded.

Patrick picked up the corned-beef cans. He stood and studied the newcomers.

Patrick eyed the weapons the soldiers carried. The shorter man had a spear with a metal tip. The other man carried a bow. A quiver of arrows hung on his back.

The soldiers' armor was made of small metal plates sewn together. The armor covered their chests and stomachs. The men wore skirts that fell to their knees. Thick leather boots came up to the tops of their shins.

"Check out their beards," Beth whispered.

The men's oily black beards were cut into a square shape. The hairs were tightly curled.

The shorter soldier with the spear stared at Patrick. The man didn't raise his weapon.

"I'm Anu," the man said. "Captain of the king's army."

"I'm Patrick," Patrick said. He raised a can of corned beef and waved it in greeting. "My cousin's name is Beth."

Captain Anu raised his spear. "Drop your weapon," the man said.

Patrick was confused. He looked at Beth. "Weapon?" he whispered.

"The corned beef," Beth said. "The soldier has never seen a can."

Patrick dropped the cans of corned beef. They landed in the sand next to the root-like formations.

The second soldier got out of his chariot. He looked a lot younger than the captain.

The soldier approached Patrick. He picked up the cans and studied them. "They are so smooth and exactly the same," the soldier said. "What are they?"

"The containers hold meat," Beth said.

Captain Anu came over to Patrick and Beth. "Where did this meat come from?" he asked.

Patrick answered honestly. "The sky," he said.

Captain Anu's expression turned to joy. "A good omen," he said.

Captain Anu now studied the cousins. "Did you and the girl come from the sky too?" he asked.

Patrick didn't know what to say at first. Then he reasoned that the Imagination Station came from the sky. Just like the gifts.

"Yes," Patrick said finally. "We came from the sky."

Both men gasped at his answer.

The soldier put down the cans of corned beef. He said, "My name is Duzi, chief scout for the king of Babylon. I offer you my services."

Captain Anu moved closer. The men knelt and bowed low in front of the cousins. The soldiers' foreheads touched the ground.

"We pay homage to you," Captain Anu said. "Welcome, children of Adad."

"Adad?" Beth asked. "Who or what is an Adad?"

The taller soldier lifted his head. "Adad is the god of lightning," he said. "There was a rainless lightning storm this morning. We came to investigate such an unusual omen."

Patrick felt uneasy. "How do you know this Adad guy sent us?" he asked.

Duzi held up the root-like formation. "This is a gift from Adad. It's made when lightning heats the sand. This is a holy place."

Beth reached for the object.

Duzi put it in her hand.

Beth inspected the formation. "It looks hollow," she said. She stuck her finger inside it. "It feels smooth like glass. But the outside is rough."

Captain Anu rose to his knees. He said, "The lightning storm is an omen."

"Omen?" Beth asked. "You used that word before. What does it mean?"

"An omen means something is going to happen. The storm was a good omen from Adad. He sent you to us," Captain Anu said. "We'll take you to the temple."

Patrick knew the lightning was from the Imagination Station. It wasn't from the false god named Adad.

He also knew he should tell the soldiers something else. He worshipped the one true God, the Creator. But he wanted out of the desert. So he kept quiet.

Patrick waved his hand. He motioned for the soldiers to stand. "Please take us to the city," he said.

"As you wish," Captain Anu said as he stood.

Duzi picked up the cans of corned beef.

He also took some of the glass made from the lightning.

Then the soldiers turned toward their chariots.

"They're not going to make us their slaves," Beth whispered to Patrick.

"At least not yet," Patrick said.

The wheels of Captain Anu's chariot were as tall as Beth. The chariot had a front panel and two side panels. The back was open.

Wood bars connected the chariot to the horse's harness. The bars kept the chariot from tipping over.

Captain Anu took Beth's arm and helped her into the chariot.

Patrick climbed in after her. "There are no seats!" he said.

The brown horse was small but beautiful. It wore a red blanket with gold trim. Its leather halter and bridle were painted with tiny gold flecks.

The captain held the reins in his hands. He flicked them, and the horse began to move. It surprised Beth how smoothly the chariot's wheels cut through the sand.

The chariots neared the city. Beth could see a wide river and a huge wall.

Duzi drove his chariot to the gate in the wall. Three soldiers opened the wooden door.

Captain Anu's chariot passed through first. Then Duzi followed.

Suddenly the desert vanished. An amazing terraced garden was inside the city walls. The top terrace was as high as a four-story building.

"Wow," Patrick whispered to Beth. "Is this the garden of Eden?"

"Wrong Bible story," Beth said. "But this garden does seem perfect."

The air smelled sweet and fresh. Trees and bushes bloomed. Green vines coiled around the ground. Birds chirped and sang. Fountains sprayed arcs of water. Small waterfalls flowed down the terraces.

The chariots moved along a dirt road. Beth craned her neck upward to see the top levels of the garden. She gazed in wonder at its beauty. And seeing the water made her thirstier.

Captain Anu pulled on the reins. The horse slowed to a walk.

"How did this garden get here?" Patrick asked the captain. "Most of the land around here has only a few trees."

"A king built it fifty years ago. His wife had grown up in the mountains," Captain Anu told them. "She didn't like the flat lands of Babylon. So the king built this garden for her. We call them the hanging gardens."

Beth remembered the statue and the king who made it.

Patrick must have too. He asked, "Was the king named Nebuchadnezzar?"

Captain Anu stopped the horse. He turned around and looked at Patrick. "You are strange children," he said. "You fall from the sky after a dry lightning storm. Yet you know nothing about our god Adad."

The captain paused and stroked his beard. "How can it be that your lips speak the name of a dead king?"

Patrick said slowly, "Hasn't everyone heard of Nebuchadnezzar?"

Captain Anu agreed. "He was a famous king," the captain said, "but he died. Later the Persians took over the land."

Beth was too thirsty to care. "Where does the water for the garden come from?" she asked. "How can I get a drink?"

"I'll show you," Captain Anu said. He flicked the horse's reins. The horse pulled the chariot around a corner. They passed a mound of bushes.

Beth could see behind the branches. Two men were dressed in dull white tunics. One was turning a wooden crank. Water poured from a wooden pipe to make a waterfall. The other slave held a bucket. He was drawing water.

Captain Anu called, "Slave, bring us some water."

The slave brought them a bucket and

some clay cups. Beth and Patrick drank four cups of water each. They said thank you and handed back the cups. The slave gave a bow.

Captain Anu snapped the reins, and the chariot moved on.

"Slaves keep the water flowing to the garden," Captain Anu said. "King Nebuchadnezzar's counselors invented a watering system. It brings water from the river. Slaves also tend the garden and keep the animals."

The chariot passed a large boulder. Beth saw movement out of the corner of her eye. She looked up. She hoped to see a monkey or a peacock.

Suddenly a lion leaped from the top of the boulder.

"Look out!" Duzi shouted.

The Gates of Babylon

The lion landed on the horse's back. Its claws dug in. The horse let out a deep moan.

The big cat clung to the horse's back. Beth screamed.

The horse bolted and the chariot jolted.

Beth fell out of the chariot and landed on the grass.

Patrick jumped after her. He landed

facedown. *Pftt!* Patrick heard an arrow zip by. He looked up.

The arrow flew past the lion's shoulder. The beast's mouth was open. Its teeth were yellow and sharp.

Duzi stood in his chariot. He was pulling his bow back to shoot another arrow.

The lion jumped off the horse. In a flash, it moved back on top of the boulder. It shook its mane and roared.

Captain Anu moved to the base of the boulder. His horse had run off. It was pulling the empty chariot down the path.

Duzi released a second arrow. *Pftt!*

It missed again.

The lion growled and swiped a huge paw at Captain Anu.

The captain dodged the claws. He raised his spear.

The lion turned and leaped off the boulder. It sped into the bushes.

Captain Anu shouted to Duzi. "Take Adad's children to safety. I'll track the beast."

The captain pulled a knife from inside his leather boot. He took his spear and climbed the boulder. He vanished into the bushes.

Patrick helped Beth stand up. They hurried to Duzi's chariot and climbed inside.

Duzi yelled, "Be off!" He snapped the reins.

The horse moved quickly. It seemed to want to get away from the danger too.

"How did that lion get in here?" Beth asked Duzi. "The city walls are really high."

"King Darius keeps a pit of lions near the garden," Duzi said. "I heard that one escaped last night when they . . ." The scout's voice trailed off.

"When they what?" Beth asked.

Duzi hesitated. He seemed uncomfortable. "When they fed the lions," he finally said.

"Why does the king keep lions?" Beth asked. "Is this a zoo?"

Duzi shook his head. "Most animals roam freely here," he said. "But the lions are kept for special events. Lion hunting at festivals is popular. The king and his guards chase one until it's killed."

"That is *so* mean," Beth said.

Patrick asked, "Why do you kill animals? Can't you just eat cake or have a parade?"

Duzi chuckled. "We do eat cake and have parades," he said. "But the lion hunts show that the king is powerful. It proves he can protect us."

"So one trapped lion against a king and his soldiers," Beth said. "That's not fair."

Beth scowled at Duzi. Then she turned to look at the gardens.

They passed over a moat and came to a fortress. Soldiers stood on the edge of a tower.

The chariot clattered down a road paved with bricks. Tall walls on both sides were covered with colorful, glazed stones.

Beth liked the artwork along the walls. Yellow, red, and white stone lions seemed to guard Babylon.

"Do these lions on the wall mean anything?" Beth asked.

"The lion is the symbol of the goddess of war," Duzi said. "Her name is Ishtar."

This gate was more ornate than the one near the hanging gardens. The city gates were beautiful and tall. The doors were made from thick cedar beams. The beams were covered in blue-and-white stone. Images of bulls and dragons decorated them.

Beth guessed there were more than a hundred of the beautiful animal figures.

Patrick asked, "What do the dragons mean?"

"The dragon represents Marduk," Duzi said. "He is the god who protects our city."

"And the bulls?" Beth asked. "They look scary."

Duzi chuckled. "You'll learn to love the bull symbol," he said. "It is yours now. The bull represents the god Adad."

Duzi blew on his horn. The city gates slowly swung open.

Beth could see men pushing on the massive cedar doors. The men. They wore the dull white tunics of slaves.

Soldiers with whips stood behind them. They forced the slaves to work. Beth knew a slave's life was a hard one. She felt sorry for the men who had to work so hard.

The chariot rolled into the city.

Beth smelled spices and roasted meat. In front of her was a crowded marketplace in a wide courtyard.

Men in bright-colored clothes and hats sold food, candles, wool, and jewelry. Women were shopping and selling wares too. They wore gold bands around their heads. The bands decorated their long hair.

Camels with goods on their backs walked through the market. Merchants led the camels as they called, "Apples, fresh from the orchard!" "Best leeks this side of the river!" "Pig's-foot lotion. Cures all ills!"

Duzi directed the horse around the marketplace.

Beth could see several structures. "What's that tall building in the middle?" she asked.

It looked like a model made out of stone Legos. Each story of the structure was larger than the one above it. And each story was a different color of the rainbow.

"It's Babylon's most ancient building," Duzi said. "The Egyptians have their great pyramids. We have our great ziggurat. We call it a platform to heaven. It's a temple to Marduk."

"Is *everything* here dedicated to the gods?" Patrick asked.

Duzi turned around. He had a puzzled look on his face. "What else is there in life but to honor the gods?" he asked. "We owe our very lives to them. Without their protection, we would surely die."

The Temple of Adad

The chariot crossed over a wide, low bridge. The river stretched out to Patrick's right and left. The water was muddy. A few long, narrow boats floated on the river. Their single white sails flapped in the wind.

Babylonian men and women hurried across the bridge. Some carried baskets. Others walked alongside donkey carts.

A few camels were laden with baskets. The animals crossed the bridge on spindly legs.

The chariot crisscrossed through straight, narrow streets. Duzi suddenly pulled back on the reins. The horse stopped moving.

"Here is your new home," Duzi said to the cousins. "The temple of Adad."

Patrick looked at the structure. The temple was part of a larger compound. A brick wall surrounded the grounds. The front gate was open.

An old man waited at the gate. He was wearing an all-white tunic. A plain gold headband held back his long white hair.

The man bowed to Duzi. "Blessings, favored servant of the king," the man said. "I'm Tanzi. I offer my service to you."

Duzi motioned for Patrick and Beth to get out of the chariot.

The cousins stepped to the ground.

The old man studied them with open curiosity. But he said nothing.

Duzi got out too. He held the reins in one hand. In his other hand was a red cloth bag.

The scout handed the chariot reins to the old man. "See that the horse is watered," he said.

The old man bowed and took the horse by its halter. The man slowly led the horse to a watering trough.

A tower stood just inside the gate. It loomed over the courtyard. Two guards stood on the top.

Patrick watched visitors and other servants mill around the courtyard. Some Babylonians were kneeling at small stone altars.

A large statue of a man was in the center of the courtyard. The man had on an upside-down bucket hat. He had a thick, square beard like other Babylonian men. He was holding a scepter.

There were carvings on the courtyard wall. They showed the man with the sun, moon, and stars above his head. Some carvings showed people bowing to the man.

Another building was attached to the courtyard. Patrick guessed it was a temple.

Just then a beautiful woman walked into the courtyard. People moved aside to let her pass.

The woman's dress was made of bright, striped fabric. She wore a large gold headdress on top of her long, dark hair. The headdress looked like a pair of giant horns.

Two men walked behind the woman. The men were dressed in striped tunics and robes. Their hats had gold trim. They wore thick gold bracelets. Their beards were so dark that Patrick could tell they were dyed.

The woman came to Duzi.

Duzi bowed to the woman. "Greetings, Anatu," he said. "May Adad find favor with you."

"And with you," Anatu said. She didn't bow in return. "What business does the king's chief scout have with Adad's priestess? I'm busy with the king's advisers." She pointed to the two men.

Duzi nodded. "I will be brief." He motioned to the cousins, and his bracelets jingled. "I bring you temple servants, children of Adad."

Anatu glanced at Patrick and Beth. Her beautiful eyes were dark, almost black. They were rimmed with gray-and-red makeup.

"Is that true?" Anatu asked. "Are you children of Adad?"

Beth said, "Duzi seems to think so."

Patrick didn't like hearing Beth tell a half truth. But he didn't tell the truth either.

Anatu seemed unimpressed with the cousins. "They have a foreign look," the priestess said to Duzi. "They aren't from Babylon. Nor Egypt."

"You're right. The children aren't from this region," Duzi said. "I found them on the Plain of Dura. They appeared right after the dry lightning storm."

Anatu's lip curled to a sneer. "The boy has pale eyes," she said. "That's a sign of weakness."

Patrick blinked. "My eyes are fine," he said.

Anatu waved her hand. "Throw the children in the river," she said. "Let them serve the god of the underworld."

Patrick's heart froze in fear. He felt Beth grab his hand. Her hand was cold.

"But there was an omen," Duzi said. "We don't want to upset Adad." He reached into his bag and took out the strange glass tube. "This was made by the morning lightning storm. The children appeared in the same holy spot."

Patrick noticed the two advisers listening intently.

Anatu took the odd formation. "I saw the storm," she said. "I was standing on top of the temple by the altar."

The woman's eyes narrowed as she studied the glass tube. She raised an eyebrow. "Are there more?" she asked Duzi.

"One more," Duzi said. "But it will be a tribute to King Darius."

She frowned for a moment. Then she turned her eyes to the cousins.

"This omen is for the girl only," Anatu said. "Take the boy away. His blue eyes frighten me. They see into the future."

One of the men said, "Perhaps he is a seer."

"Then King Darius will want to consult with him," Anatu said.

Beth gasped. "No!" she said. "Patrick and I must stay together. If he goes, I go."

Patrick felt Duzi's hands grab his shoulders. "Stop!" Patrick shouted.

Beth watched as Patrick kicked Duzi's shins. But the scout's thick leather boots protected his legs.

Duzi lifted Patrick off the ground. "Put me

down!" Patrick shouted. He flailed his arms and legs.

Duzi carried Patrick out of the courtyard and through the gate.

Beth began to run after them. But Anatu grabbed Beth's forearm. The priestess squeezed hard.

"Ow," Beth said. "Let go!" Beth thought her bone would snap.

Anatu laughed and gripped Beth tighter.

"Duzi!" Beth shouted. She tried to pull her arm free.

Anatu held it fast.

"Please come back!" Beth called after Duzi and Patrick. "Don't leave me here."

Beth's voice echoed off the stone walls.

Anatu laughed again. The priestess locked eyes with Beth. The woman's dark eyes were beautiful. But they seemed empty.

"You have a choice," Anatu said. "If you obey me, you can become a temple priestess. If you don't obey me, you'll become a temple *sacrifice*."

Anatu shook Beth's arm. "Do you understand?"

Beth slowly nodded. She bit her lip to keep tears from flowing.

"You will learn your place," Anatu said. The priestess let go of Beth.

Beth rubbed her aching arm. She glared at Anatu.

But Anatu was no longer looking at Beth. The priestess was striding across the courtyard. The two men followed her toward the temple. The people in the courtyard moved back to give them room.

"Tanzi!" Anatu shouted. "Come here, you good-for-nothing dog."

Inside the Palace

At the palace, Patrick and Duzi got out of the chariot. Patrick took a deep breath to calm down. He followed Duzi inside.

The palace rooms were large and drafty. Glazed tiles covered the walls and floor. Patrick felt cold.

Carvings and paintings decorated the walls. Most of the images were of battle scenes. Some of the pictures showed animals running or slaves working.

There was a map of the world. It showed the earth as flat. Patrick smiled. There was also a chart. It showed the cycle of the moon. Was it a calendar?

A few of the pictures had writing near them. The Babylonian writing had dashes and sideways *v* shapes: > or <. In some places, the writing looked like bird tracks.

Tables held sculptures and painted tiles. Some tables had clay tablets stacked underneath them.

Patrick went to a table and picked up a tablet. He touched the strange writing on it.

"Do you know how to read and write?" Duzi asked.

Patrick nodded.

Duzi said, "Perhaps you can become a scribe."

No way, Patrick thought. He didn't want to sit at a desk. He carefully set the tablet down.

"Can't I become a scout for the king, like you?" Patrick asked. He wanted to race in a chariot and carry a spear.

Duzi smiled. "You'll live longer as a scribe," he said. "Or a seer. For either profession, the king will have to appoint you."

Duzi walked toward a narrow hallway. "Come with me," he said. "You need to wash your face. You must look presentable when you see the king."

Duzi led Patrick into a large room. It had lots of low beds. The frames were made of thick poles. Ropes crisscrossed the poles to form a mattress.

Duzi pointed to a door at the end of the

room. He said, "You can find water to bathe with in there."

Patrick hurried to the bathroom.

Beth stood alone in the courtyard, thinking. She planned to run away as soon as it was dark.

Tanzi appeared at her side. He gently put a hand on her elbow. "Anatu wishes you to come with me," he said.

Beth saw a sun and a moon tattooed on the back of his hand.

"Are you a slave?" she asked.

Tanzi nodded. "I bear the mark of Adad," he said. "I have served him since I was five."

"So young!" Beth said. "Were your parents slaves too?"

The old man shook his head. "My home country is Syria," he said. "King Nebuchadnezzar attacked my city. My parents died in the battle. I was taken captive and brought to Babylon."

Tanzi steered Beth in the direction of the temple. "Come with me to the temple," he said. "Anatu needs us."

Tanzi led Beth through the courtyard past the statue and altars.

They came to the temple. It had two stories. A wide set of stairs was on the outside of the building. The stairs led to the top floor and the roof.

"The priests and priestesses may come inside," Tanzi said. "We are their servants. And so we're allowed to enter too."

Tanzi gingerly climbed the stairs.

Beth followed Tanzi step by slow step.

They stopped at a small door halfway up the stairs.

Tanzi pushed open the door. He motioned for Beth to go inside.

Beth looked around. There was nothing special inside the temple. It was just a beautiful home. All of the walls were covered in colorful glazed stone.

At the back was a kitchen with a fireplace. There was a low bed. In one corner was a table. It had odd musical instruments on it.

The rugs were wool. They were woven with images of the sun and moon.

"Who lives here?" Beth asked.

"You are daft, child," Tanzi said. He lightly slapped the back of her head. "Don't ask such questions in front of Anatu."

Beth rubbed her head. "I've never been

to Babylon before," she said. "How am I supposed to know who lives here?"

"Adad dwells here," Tanzi said. "That's why it's called the Adad temple."

A chill went up Beth's spine. "You think he's real?" she asked the old servant.

"Of course," Tanzi said.

"Have you seen him?" Beth asked.

Tanzi shook his head. "No one sees the gods," he said. "Kings are the gods we can see. They are the ones who protect us."

Beth was confused. "So I'm supposed to serve a god named Adad. Everyone thinks he lives here. But he isn't really here."

"Ah," Tanzi said. "But he is here. Adad speaks to us through signs and omens. You'll help Anatu with that."

"What signs and omens?" Beth said.

"You'll see," Tanzi said. "Anatu will teach you."

Beth wanted nothing to do with the angry priestess. She needed to get out of there soon.

"Here is Anatu's room," Tanzi said. He limped inside.

Beth followed. The room was small but elegant. There was a makeup table, and soft cushions were arranged on a low couch. Rugs hung on the wall and lay on the floor.

Beth moved to some long, thin curtain panels and pushed them aside. They covered a window. The window overlooked a street outside the temple.

Tanzi said, "To look like a priestess, you need a headdress." He picked up a headdress similar to the one Anatu wore. It was a gold hat shaped like bull horns.

Beth scowled. "I don't want to wear that," she said. "I'll look like the princess of cows."

Tanzi frowned. "It is an honor to be a child of Adad," he said.

I'll pretend I'm in a school play, Beth thought. *It's just a costume. The headdress doesn't mean anything.* But still, she didn't think Eugene or Mr. Whittaker would like her wearing it. It gave her an uneasy feeling.

Tanzi gently placed the headdress on Beth's head. He took a comb from the table and smoothed her hair. Then he placed pins in her hair so the headdress would stay on.

Suddenly Beth heard the temple door swing open. Sandals slapped on the tile floor.

"Where are you, Tanzi?" Anatu shouted. "We're at the holy altar. Hurry up!"

The palace bathroom was large. It had room for at least ten men. But Patrick was alone. He washed his face, hands, and feet in a small fountain.

Patrick heard a hissing noise. He turned around. The helicopter Imagination Station stood in the middle of the bathroom. It was as if the machine could read his mind. He wanted to leave Babylon, but he couldn't.

The Imagination Station's white paint seemed to be glowing. Patrick touched the machine's side. It was warm. The door automatically opened.

Patrick stared at the empty seats and the red button on the dashboard. He hesitated. He didn't want to get inside without Beth.

"Hurry up," Duzi called. "King Darius is waiting."

Patrick slowly moved away from the Imagination Station. He turned to leave the bathroom. The machine hissed.

Patrick looked back over his shoulder. The Imagination Station was gone.

He felt a sinking feeling in his stomach.

He had never ignored the Imagination Station before. He wondered, *What if it doesn't come back?*

The Advisers' Plan

Tanzi picked up a basket from a table near the door. The slave and Beth left the temple and climbed the stairs outside.

A heavy scent filled the air on the temple roof. It reminded Beth of a candle shop.

Anatu and the king's two advisers were standing near a great stone altar. They were whispering. The men were each holding a small clay jar.

A low wall surrounded the rooftop. There were a few beautiful stone benches here and there. Carvings of the sun, moon, and stars were on everything. Other strange symbols were carved on the ground.

Along one wall Beth saw dozens of wood cages. White doves cooed from inside their small homes.

The advisers paid her no attention at all. They kept on talking in low voices. Beth overheard words like "New law." "Worship only the king." "Trap."

Anatu suddenly looked up. She scowled at Beth and Tanzi.

The priestess said, "Tanzi, prepare the incense on the holy altar."

Tanzi bowed. He motioned to Beth to come with him.

"Those men are two of King Darius's

top advisers," Tanzi whispered. "They are Persian, like the king. The taller one is Frava. The other is Katav. Show them respect or they'll have you killed."

Beth gulped.

Tanzi put a hand under her chin. He looked her in the eyes. "It is *very* important to obey Anatu," he said. "Do whatever she says. It is your sacred duty."

Beth nodded. Her golden horns slid back and forth on her head.

Tanzi led Beth toward the altar. The heavy smell grew stronger.

Beth saw small pots on the altar. They had shavings of red bark in them. The bark was mixed with oil.

Tanzi added more bark and oil from the basket.

Frava and Katav were moving toward the

altar with Anatu. They still carried their clay jars.

Beth could now hear their hushed voices more clearly. Frava said, "If our plan works, he will be executed. Our power will increase."

"Your plan is clever," Anatu said. "The king's own law will be used against his favorite adviser."

Then Frava and Katav laughed. They sounded mean.

Beth shivered.

"Let us get on with the ceremony of blessing," Katav said. "We need to return to King Darius's court. We'll present the new law to him today."

Anatu said, "Of course. Let us offer our gifts to Adad."

The priestess stood before the altar. She

raised her palms to the sky. The men did the same thing.

"O Adad," Anatu prayed, "Lord of prophecy who lives in the shining heavens. Accept our incense. We lift up our hands. May justice crown our request."

Anatu stopped praying. She turned to Beth. "We will offer a blood sacrifice to Adad," the priestess said. "Girl, go bring me a dove."

"I can't do this," Beth said. "I can't worship a false god."

Anatu raised an eyebrow. The priestess said, "Did I just hear you say 'false god'?"

Beth reached for the headdress on her head. She pulled out the hairpins.

"I not only *can't* do this," Beth said, "but I *won't*. I'm not a child of Adad." She took off the headdress

and threw it on the ground. It made a loud clanging sound.

"Be careful what you say, girl," Tanzi said. Worry filled his voice. He was wringing his hands.

"I won't bring you a dove. You'll just kill it," Beth said. "And I won't pray to any god except the one true God."

Anatu's face showed mock interest. "And who is this one true God?" she asked. "You're risking your life for Him."

"He's the God of the Jews," Beth said.

Anatu looked bored. She glanced at her dress and brushed off a small piece of dirt. "The Jews are a scraggly bunch. They're captives now. That shows their God is weak. He can't protect them."

Frava and Katav exchanged glances.

"We've heard of the Jewish God." Katav

said. "He is the one our enemy worships. But we don't fear Him."

"Then this girl is our enemy too," Anatu said. "She deserves death."

Beth felt her heart sink to her stomach. She opened her mouth to say something. But her mouth was too dry.

Tanzi raised a hand to Anatu. "O priestess," he said, "I beg permission to speak."

A sudden warm wind swept across the rooftop. It filled Beth with hope.

Anatu's long hair danced in the breeze. She didn't say anything. She seemed to be in a trance. She stood still with her arms lifted high.

Tanzi went on talking. "I was alive when three men named Shadrach, Meshach, and Abednego were living," he said. "Forty years ago King Nebuchadnezzar tried to burn them alive. But their God performed a miracle to save them."

Frava said, "Enough, old man. We didn't come here for a history lesson. We came here for the favor of Adad. We want his blessing on our plan."

Katav poured the contents of his jar on the altar.

The altar glowed with orange-and-black flames. The flames burned off thick, gray smoke.

Frava said, "Priestess, continue with the prayers. We have offered sesame oil."

"No," Anatu said. "I've received a message from Adad." She lowered her arms. "He said that the God of the Jews is powerful. Do not bring harm to His followers."

Katav laughed. "I don't need Adad's help. Or the help of any god." He looked at Frava.

"Let's go to the royal court. The king will sign the decree today. By noon tomorrow, our enemy will be dead."

Frava pointed a finger at Anatu. He said, "You'll regret listening to this girl." He threw his jar on the ground. It crashed and broke into pieces. The oil seeped into the stone floor. "We'll send the tower guards to arrest her."

The men walked down the stairs and disappeared from view.

Beth stood in stunned silence.

"Leave at once, girl," Anatu said. "If Katav and Frava find you in Babylon, they'll arrest you, or worse."

Beth said, "Thank you, but I—"

Tanzi cut her off. "Go before she changes her mind."

Beth turned and hurried down the stairs.

Two Kings

Duzi led Patrick to the door of the king's court. The wood doors were carved with lions. The lions looked like the ones on the city gate.

Just then guards opened the door to the court.

Patrick stepped inside the spacious hall. The area was filled with statues and pictures on the wall.

A man was sitting at the head of a long table. The table was filled with food. Several men also sat at the banquet. Most of the men looked rich and well fed.

The man at the head of the table wore a gold crown. Patrick guessed that man was King Darius.

Patrick glanced at the goblets and plates of food. There were jugs and baskets of flatbread too. It seemed that he and Duzi had come during a feast.

"Anu!" Duzi said. He marched toward the table.

The captain stood and moved toward Duzi. Captain Anu gave Duzi several backslaps. Then the captain slapped Patrick on the back in welcome.

"What happened to the lion?" Patrick asked.

"I captured it, of course," Captain Anu said. "Did you doubt me?"

Duzi laughed. "Yes," he said. "I thought you would be tracking it for days."

Captain Anu smiled and said, "The lion can do no harm. It's back in the pit."

A thin man was sitting near the king. He was the only man without a beard.

The beardless man called to Duzi, "What news do you have, chief scout?"

"I bring the king great news from Adad," Duzi said loudly.

The men at the table perked up. They stopped eating.

Duzi approached the king. He opened his red bag and took out a piece of glass. He also pulled out the cans of corned beef.

Duzi put the objects on the table in front of King Darius. The scout looked at the men. "Great leaders of Babylon," Duzi said, "let me tell you an amazing tale . . ."

Patrick listened as Duzi described the lightning storm. He told how he found Patrick and Beth in the desert. He held up the glass object formed by the lighting.

The king saw it and smiled with approval. "I'll put that in the royal museum," he said.

Then Duzi continued his tale. The scout was a good storyteller. He ended his story by saying, "The priestess Anatu said the boy's eyes are remarkable. He may be a seer."

King Darius said, "Child of Adad, come to me."

Patrick cringed at being called Adad's child. But he didn't correct the king. He walked toward the head of the table. He saw the meat, sesame oil, and cakes set before the men. The food smelled delicious.

But the thin man wasn't eating. His plate hadn't been touched.

Patrick stood before Darius. The king studied Patrick's face. He looked deep into Patrick's eyes. "Tell me, child," he asked, "what is the future of the great city of Babylon?"

"I think . . . umm," Patrick said. He tried to remember some history from school and his adventures. "The Romans will basically take over everywhere."

"The Romans?" King Darius said. He leaned forward. "I must prepare the city for battle. How long until they come?"

Patrick shrugged. "It's probably sometime in BC," he said. Patrick hoped he was right.

"BC?" the king asked.

"I think it means 'before Christ,' " Patrick said. "Or maybe it means something in Latin." Then he said with confidence, "I'm sure the Romans will invade before Jesus Christ is born."

A tall, heavy man with a very long beard stood. "Your highness," he said, "this boy knows nothing. Rome is but a small country. Rome's king is weak. This cannot be. It's a trick."

Patrick wished Eugene were with him. He would know how to explain things.

King Darius smoothed his beard. "This is strange news indeed," he said.

The beardless, thin man stood now too. "Who is this Jesus?" he asked. "His name sounds like a Hebrew word."

"I *think* He's a Hebrew," Patrick said. "Jesus is the king of the Jews."

At this the other men at the table began to laugh. Some pointed fingers at Patrick. One man was laughing so hard that he choked.

"What's so funny?" Patrick asked the men.

A third man stood. He was wearing purple robes. "*I* am king of the Jews," he said. "I am Jehoiachin from the line of King David. One day the holy city, Jerusalem, will be great again."

"Oh . . ." Patrick began. "Jesus isn't just *a* king. He's the Messiah—"

The tall man said, "Enough talk. The boy should be banished."

King Darius nodded. "Remove this fool from my court," he said. The king picked up a fork and stabbed a chicken leg.

The feast began again. The men ate thick slabs of meat. The tall man picked up a goblet, took a swig of wine, swallowed, and then burped.

Patrick felt Duzi's hand on his shoulder. The scout leaned in and whispered, "It's best we go." Duzi picked up the cans of corned beef. He put them back in the red bag.

Duzi and Patrick began to leave the great hall. Patrick's shoulders slumped. His eyes stung. He was afraid he might cry.

"Wait," a voice said from behind them. "I would hear more from the boy about the Messiah."

Daniel

Beth paused on the fifth stair down from the temple roof. She looked into the courtyard.

Her hopes sank. She saw one of the guards from the tower. He was searching in the center of the courtyard. Beth thought that Katav and Frava must have sent the guards.

She gasped. The second guard was now headed up the stairs.

Beth ducked inside the temple and

rushed to Anatu's bedroom. She looked out the window. No one was in the street below.

Beth yanked the curtains down with one swift pull. She tied the lengths of curtain together. It made a long rope. She double-checked each knot with a tug. Then she tied one end of the curtain rope around a leg of the bed.

"She went this way," a voice shouted. The voice was coming from inside the temple.

Beth quickly threw the rest of the curtains out the window.

This has to hold, she thought.

Beth sat on the windowsill and then turned stomach-side-down. She held tightly to the curtains as she lowered herself. She looked down. She was halfway to the ground.

Suddenly she felt herself being lifted. She looked up.

An angry soldier was pulling the curtain rope. He was reeling her back toward the window. "I've got you now, traitor," he said.

Beth bit her lip and closed her eyes. She let go of the rope and fell to the ground. The jolt of the landing stung her feet. But the pain ebbed quickly.

She ran away from the temple as fast as she could.

The thin man from the banquet wore an orange robe. His hair was all white. His eyes were bright. He seemed amazingly fit for an old man. The man said, "This way. Follow me."

The man led Patrick and Duzi out of the great hall.

Duzi paused in the corridor. "I must

attend to my duties. I need to patrol the palace grounds," he said to the man. "Will you take charge of the boy for the rest of the day?"

The man said, "I will accept him as my servant. But first he must answer two questions correctly."

Patrick felt uneasy. What if the man asked more questions about the future?

"Name them," Duzi said.

The man looked Patrick over with concerned brown eyes. "You are a worshipper of the God of Moses?" he asked Patrick.

Patrick nodded.

"Then why did you break the first commandment?" the man asked. There was a sharpness to his tone.

Patrick hung his head. "You shall have no

other gods before Me," he said, mumbling. "I let them think I was a child of Adad. I was afraid they would make me a slave. I was a coward."

The man lifted Patrick's chin. "Better to be a slave for the almighty God," he said, "than to be a king for any other god."

Duzi slapped Patrick on the back. "That's it then," he said. "You'll find your way into the king's court yet."

Duzi bowed to the thin man. He said, "Thank you, O wise one."

"Only God is wise," the man said. "Call me Daniel."

The city walls were high. Beth couldn't see around them. She turned a corner. The street looked oddly familiar. Was she traveling in circles?

Beth had to find the palace. She peered around the corner of a wall. There were no soldiers.

Beth heard the clomping of animal hooves. She looked behind her.

A wagon had turned onto the street. Its wheels squished thin track marks in the dirt. The wagon was filled with baskets of pistachio nuts. A woman sat on the wagon bench. She was driving a team of donkeys.

Beth guessed the woman was going to the marketplace. Beth squatted low and walked alongside the wagon to hide.

Just then one of the soldiers turned the corner. He looked to his left. Then he looked to his right.

He's searching for me, Beth thought.

Dear God, she prayed, *hide me!*

The New Law

Patrick followed Daniel through the halls of the palace. They came to a courtyard with a giant fountain in the center. The fountain waters flowed into a large flower garden.

The courtyard was surrounded by two-story buildings. The area reminded Patrick of a motel. The doors all faced the courtyard. Shutters covered the windows above the doors.

Daniel led Patrick through one of the doorways. The first floor of Daniel's house was simple. There was a small, low couch. A basket of scrolls sat next to it. Wool rugs covered the tile floor.

Daniel went up a narrow staircase at the back of the room. Patrick followed him.

The top floor was open. A thick rug was in the center of the room. A large, uncovered window faced the courtyard.

"Why did you take the shutters off the window?" Patrick asked.

"This window faces Jerusalem," Daniel said. "The city and the Temple lie in rubble. But still, I want nothing to come between me and the holy city."

Patrick looked out the window over the palace walls. He could see a small portion of the horizon.

Patrick turned around. Daniel was kneeling on the rug. He seemed to be praying.

Patrick knelt too. He started to pray. He asked God to forgive him for pretending to be Adad's child.

The wagon passed by the marketplace and kept going. Beth realized it must be headed to the palace kitchen.

Beth sneaked inside the palace gates next to the wagon. The wagon stopped near the palace building at the back. Beth quickly picked up a basket of pistachio nuts. She carried the basket into the kitchen.

Beth passed marble tables covered with pots and knives. Large chunks of meat were roasting over open stone fire pits. A woman was chopping figs and dates.

The woman looked up and pointed to a table. "Put the pistachios over there," she said.

Beth set the basket down.

"You look too fancy for kitchen help," the woman said.

Beth looked down at her purple dress. "Oh," she said. "It's a nice dress in case I need to go to the king's court."

"Well, hurry then," the woman said. "The king's banquet is over now. Bring in the dirty dishes. Don't drop any serving trays. And don't steal any food."

Beth nodded. "Right," she said. "Please remind me where the king's hall is."

The woman sighed. "The help has never been the same since the Persians came," she said as if to herself. She motioned with her head toward a doorway. "Go through there. Take two rights and then a left."

Beth hurried through the door. *If I can find the king*, she thought, *maybe I'll find Patrick!*

Beth followed the woman's directions. She ended up in the doorway of a great hall. Several thick plants in enormous bronze pots covered the servants' entrance.

Beth stood behind the plants. She peeked through the leaves and looked around the vast room.

About ten men were seated at a long table. The men leaned back in their comfortable chairs. A few were holding goblets filled with wine. Plates were stacked high with piles of food scraps.

Beth recognized Captain Anu. His back was toward her.

A bearded man with a crown sat at the head of the table. He wore a fine robe. The man was holding a clay tablet. He set it down on the table. Then he pressed something into the clay.

Frava was seated on the king's right. Katav was seated on his left.

There was no sign of Patrick.

Beth wanted to hear what was said. She sneaked to the end of the table. She picked up a metal platter. It had a pig carcass on it. She lifted the platter high to hide her face.

The men ignored her.

Katav stood. He picked up the clay tablet and cleared his throat.

"A new law has just been signed," he read. "A decree that will bring honor to King Darius. No person is allowed to pray to any god or being other than King Darius. This decree shall last for thirty days."

Beth wondered if all the temples would close down. Anatu would hate that.

"If anyone disobeys this law," Katav said, "that person will be fed to the lions."

Beth suddenly realized which Bible story she was in. Frava and Katav were plotting to have a man named Daniel killed.

Beth felt weak. She quickly put the metal platter down. It hit the table with a clang.

All the men turned to look at her.

Katav stood. He pointed at her. "I know that girl!" he shouted. "Arrest her! She doesn't worship Babylonian gods! She's a traitor."

Beth turned and ran toward the servants' entrance. She made it to the large plants. Then she bumped into something solid. She felt arms encircle her.

Beth looked up at her captor.

"Hello," Duzi said. "You're a long way from Adad's temple."

King Darius's Regret

Daniel finished praying. He stood and walked back down the stairs.

Patrick followed the old man to the living room.

Daniel sat on the low couch. "Tell me more about this Messiah who is to come," he said.

Patrick sat on a wool rug on the floor. "Jesus was—or will be—born in

Bethlehem," he said. "His mother was the Virgin Mary."

Daniel's eyes grew wide. "The prophet Isaiah foretold such an event," he said. Daniel reached for one of the scrolls in the basket. He unrolled the paper and read, "'Therefore the Lord himself will give you a sign. Behold, the virgin shall conceive and bear a son, and shall call his name Immanuel.'"

Patrick told Daniel what he remembered about Jesus' miracles. The old man listened carefully. He seemed glad when Patrick said that Jesus healed blind and deaf people.

"Isaiah said that would be a sign too," Daniel said. "Go on."

Patrick paused. "Before I tell you more about Jesus, I have a question for you," he said.

"I will answer truthfully," Daniel said.

"It's about the day of the fiery furnace," Patrick said. "King Nebuchadnezzar tried to kill your three friends."

Daniel cast a glance at Patrick. "They were spared," he said. "God saved them. They became famous. King Nebuchadnezzar gave them honor. But they have since died."

"Why weren't you with them on that day?" Patrick asked.

"I remember it well," Daniel said. He rubbed his forehead. "King Jehoiachin was in jail then. He asked me to take a message to the few Jews left in Jerusalem. I was traveling outside the city that month."

"Why don't all the Jews go back to Jerusalem?" Patrick asked.

"The leaders of Babylon won't let us," Daniel said. "And God is punishing the Jews for worshipping other gods."

Daniel reached for another scroll. He unrolled it and said, "The prophet Jeremiah said our exile would be for seventy years. There are a few more years to wait in Babylon before we return home. Until then the Jews are to serve the Babylonians well."

Daniel pointed to a portion of the scroll.

A knock on the door startled Patrick.

Daniel called, "Enter in peace."

Captain Anu came through the door. "Come quickly," the soldier said to Daniel. "The king requires your presence in the great hall."

"Oh?" Daniel said.

Captain Anu looked at Patrick. "The boy's cousin is causing trouble," he said. "Her words have distressed the king."

Beth sat at the king's banquet table. Duzi sat next to her as her guard.

Beth watched Patrick enter the great hall. Captain Anu and an old man followed him.

Beth jumped out of her chair in excitement. She ran toward the old man. "Are you Daniel?" she cried. "You're one of my favorite Bible heroes!" Beth threw her arms around him.

Daniel patted her head. "I have no idea what a Bible is," he said kindly. "And I'm no hero. Salvation comes only from the Lord God. Do you also know about God and the law of Moses?" Daniel asked.

Beth nodded.

Duzi joined the group. He slapped Captain Anu on the back.

Captain Anu said, "These two children have caused a ruckus today."

Patrick leaned toward Beth. "The king is crying," he said. "Why?"

Beth let go of Daniel. She turned around and looked at the king.

King Darius's head was in his hands. He was quietly weeping.

"He made a HUGE mistake," Beth said. "He signed a bad law. And not even he can undo it. That's the way the Persians do it."

"So?" Patrick said.

"So that law will get Daniel into trouble," Beth said. "And I told the king he was silly. He shouldn't have signed it."

"I can't see Daniel breaking any laws," Patrick said. "What is this new law?"

"A good question," Daniel said. "What new law governs Babylon?"

Duzi said, "You should hear it from Frava and Katav."

The group moved close to the table.

Katav held up a clay tablet. "King Darius just signed this," Katav said. He pointed to the bottom of the tablet. A lion's head was impressed on the clay. "It has the royal seal on it."

Daniel walked over to Katav. He took the clay tablet and read it.

"It says no one is to pray to any god or being except for King Darius," Daniel said. "Anyone who does will be thrown into the lions' pit." Daniel slowly scanned the room. He looked all the king's men in the eyes. "So be it."

The king stood. "I forgot about you, my friend," he said. King Darius reached a hand toward Daniel.

Daniel didn't reach back.

The king dropped his hand. "Daniel," the king said, "would you please not pray to your god for thirty days? You're my chief adviser. I need you."

Daniel lowered his head. He didn't answer. He turned away from the king's table. "Children of the one true God," he said, "come with me. We have something important to do."

Daniel walked out of the banquet room. Patrick and Beth followed.

Behind them, the men were still talking. Beth heard Frava laugh. She looked over her shoulder.

Katav said, "Daniel is so predictable. He prays three times a day no matter what." He turned to Captain Anu and said, "Arrest Daniel when he dares to worship the Jewish God."

13

The Open Window

Daniel went straight to his house and up the stairs. Patrick watched him kneel on the rug in his second-floor room.

Daniel began to pray softly.

Beth stood in the doorway watching. "Isn't he at least going to close the window?" Beth quietly asked Patrick. "He'll be seen."

"I think that's the point," Patrick whispered.

Patrick knelt next to Daniel. Beth knelt next to Patrick. They all bowed toward Jerusalem and the open window.

Patrick knew anyone walking through the garden below would see them. And only a few minutes later, someone did.

Patrick heard the front door open. Then he heard footsteps come up the stairs.

Someone was standing in the doorway.

Patrick turned around. He saw Captain Anu and Duzi.

"You didn't knock this time," Patrick said.

The captain frowned. "Daniel wasn't under arrest last time," he said. He motioned with his head toward the old man.

Daniel was still praying silently.

Beth looked out the window. "There's a crowd in the courtyard," she said. "And an empty wagon with two horses."

Patrick went to the window and looked down. A lot of men wearing upside-down bucket hats were gathered in the garden. Several women were there too. They all stared up at Daniel's window.

Katav and Frava stood near the fountain. Their dark beards covered their mouths, but Patrick could see they were smiling.

The wagon was empty. He wondered what it was being used for.

"At least there are no TV reporters," Patrick whispered to Beth.

Captain Anu cleared his throat. The cousins turned around.

"By a decree signed by King Darius," he said, "I hereby arrest Daniel, Patrick, and Beth for praying to the Jewish God. The three of you are guilty of treason."

Daniel stood. "I will never stop serving

the almighty God. But I'm guilty of
nothing. Take me as your prisoner. I'm
ready." Daniel walked out the door with
Captain Anu.

Duzi said, "I'll have to take you two in
as well. Everyone in the courtyard saw you
praying toward Jerusalem."

Patrick heard a hum and some crackles.
The Imagination Station was appearing.
He looked at Beth. Panic was in her eyes.

"We're going to be arrested," Patrick said
to Duzi. "May we have a minute alone?"

"As you wish," Duzi said and then turned.
"I'll be waiting downstairs." He left the room.

Patrick studied the white Imagination
Station. It was glowing.

"It looks like a ghost ship," Beth said.
"What's it doing here? We came in the other
machine."

"This one appeared earlier today," Patrick said. "I ignored it because you weren't with me. Let's go before it disappears."

Patrick sat down inside the machine. The seat was tingly with static electricity. His hand hovered over the red button.

Beth stood still. She was holding the yellow gizmo in her hand. "It's flashing yellow," she said. "I think it's measuring something from the machine."

"It's probably just electric current," Patrick said. "Let's go or we may be stuck here forever."

Beth said, "We left Eugene when he needed us. I'm not leaving Daniel too." She turned and went out the door.

Patrick sighed. He got out of the machine.

It vanished with a sizzle and a flash.

The Arrest

Beth met Duzi downstairs in Daniel's living room. Captain Anu was there with Daniel.

The old man's wrists had been tied. He held the palms of his hands together close to his chest. It looked as if he was praying.

Daniel was silent.

Beth knew he would never protest. But she would. "Stop treating Daniel like a criminal!" she said. "He's not going to run away. Untie him."

"I can't take that chance," Captain Anu said. He held up some rope. "Sorry about this," he said.

Beth held out her hands. Captain Anu tied the ropes tightly around her wrists.

Patrick came down the stairs. Captain Anu bound his wrists too.

"This isn't right," Patrick said. "Daniel is loyal to the king. Everyone knows that."

Beth said, "He just wants freedom to worship God."

"He's free to worship the god Darius as much as he likes," Captain Anu said. "It's the law." The captain ushered Daniel out the front door.

The people in the courtyard saw them. They started to chant. "Kill the Jews," they shouted. "Cleanse the city of traitors."

Beth watched Katav and Frava leave the group. They hurried toward the royal banquet hall. No doubt they would tell the king about the arrest. And they would smile while telling him.

Captain Anu walked to the wagon. Duzi shouted at the people to stay back.

Patrick, Beth, and Daniel climbed in the back of the wagon. Captain Anu sat on the bench in the front.

The captain flicked the reins, and the horses moved.

"This is a prison wagon," Patrick said. "We don't even get a chariot this time."

Beth recognized one of the horses. It had scratch marks on its back. "Are we going to be fed to the lion?" she asked the captain. "You know, the same lion that attacked your horse?"

"Yes," the captain said. "You'll go to the lion pit. That lion and three others live in it."

"Four lions," Beth said. Her heart sank.

The wagon took the prisoners out of the palace. It wound its way back toward the hanging gardens.

Patrick thought the gardens didn't look so beautiful anymore. The sun was setting. It cast long, dark shadows over everything.

The trip to the lions' pit went quickly. No one spoke.

The wagon stopped near a wide walkway.

Captain Anu got out of the wagon. Then he motioned for Beth, Patrick, and Daniel to get out.

The captain looked at Patrick. "If you vow to worship King Darius," Captain Anu said,

"I'll ask the king to pardon you children. I'll say that Daniel forced you to bow toward Jerusalem."

"That's a lie," Patrick said. "I worshipped God because I wanted to."

The captain turned to Beth. He gave her a questioning glance.

"I can't deny my God either," Beth said. "Take us to the lions."

"You are courageous fools," the captain said. There was pity in his voice.

"They are faithful," Daniel said. "God won't abandon them."

Patrick felt his heart warm at Daniel's words.

Captain Anu led the prisoners down a pathway with a low wall on one side. Now Patrick could hear the growls of the lions. He could smell them too.

Beth suddenly gasped. She leaned over the wall and pointed. "There's the pit!"

Patrick looked over the wall. A metal grate was over the top of the pit. He could see four lions in the den. Their giant paws made no noise as they paced the length of the den.

Daniel made no effort to look over the wall.

The sound of a chariot caught Patrick's attention. He turned and looked down the road. Two horses were pulling a fast-moving chariot. An umbrella was perched over the riders.

"That's Duzi driving," Beth said. "I think the others are Katav, Frava, and the king."

Patrick felt a tug on the rope.

"Let's get this over with," Captain Anu said. "It's best not to linger."

The captain led them off the pathway.
A large boulder was leaning against a wall.
Captain Anu moved it with a mighty push.

Now Patrick could see a stairway leading
to the pit. The prisoners walked down the
stone steps.

Suddenly Duzi was there on the stairs.
He was carrying the red bag.

"I'll take it from here," he said to Captain
Anu. "I'd like to say good-bye."

The captain nodded. "That's it, then," he
said and walked back up the stairs.

When Captain Anu was out of sight, Duzi
spoke. "Let me have your wrists," he said.
Patrick offered the scout his hand. Duzi cut
the ropes with a short knife.

Beth held out her hands, and the ropes
were cut.

Daniel paid no attention at first.

"You should face the lions as a free man," Duzi said to Daniel.

Daniel held out his hands. "Thank you," he said. Then he walked to the bottom of the stairs. He stopped at the gate.

"Here, be quick," Duzi whispered to Patrick. "Take these objects that fell from the sky. They're yours."

Duzi put one of the corned-beef cans in Patrick's hands. He gave the other to Beth.

Then Duzi offered them a small burlap pouch. "There's sleeping powder inside," he said. "Mix it with the meat and feed it to the lions. Their hunger will be satisfied. Then they'll fall asleep."

Patrick held the can for a second. Then he shook his head. "It's a great idea, Duzi," he said. "And you're a good friend. But we have to face the lions without this."

Patrick handed the can back to Duzi. So did Beth.

Duzi's face turned pale.

Beth said, "Don't worry. The God of the Jews will save us."

"And what if he doesn't?" Duzi said.

Patrick took a deep breath. Then he said, "It's better to be a child of God and die than to live a faithless life."

Daniel pushed open the gate. He walked inside the lion pit.

Patrick took Beth's hand. "It's time," he said.

They walked inside the den together. Patrick heard the gate shut. He pulled Beth next to the wall.

"May your God be as faithful as you are," Duzi said. Then he turned and walked up the stairs.

The Angel

The lions were at the far side of the pit. Beth heard voices coming from above. She looked up through the metal grate. The Babylonians were leaning over the wall looking into the pit. The king was obviously upset. Tears streamed down his face. His hands were clutched against his chest.

Frava and Katav were both smiling in their mean way.

Captain Anu peered over the wall too.

"I can't watch," the king said. He turned away.

"Let's leave then," Captain Anu said to the king. "The stone is blocking the stairway entrance. They can't escape."

The faces were gone in a moment. Beth turned her attention back to the lions.

Beth recognized the lion from earlier. He was a male with a full, thick mane. The other three were lionesses. *Great*, Beth thought. *Females are the better hunters.*

Daniel stepped in front of the cousins. "Stay behind me," he said. He stretched out his arms as if to push the lions away.

The male lion roared. The deep, angry sound echoed off the walls. Its jaws opened wide enough to swallow Beth's entire head.

Beth's heart began to race. She felt faint with fear as she silently prayed.

The females crept forward. They stared at her with dark, unblinking eyes.

The male crouched. He was focused on Daniel. Beth could see his muscles tense.

The lion sprang.

"No!" Beth shouted.

Suddenly the den filled with a white light. Beth put her arm up to shield her eyes.

"Look," Patrick shouted. "The fourth man!"

Beth squinted. She could see the man clearly. His beauty was stunning. He had the strength of a warrior and the grace of a dancer. His face was full of peace and fury at the same time.

The man leaped on the beast. He wrapped his arms around the jaws and shut the lion's mouth.

A female lion rushed at the man. He threw the male into her path. The beast's body knocked the female against the wall.

Two lionesses charged Daniel. The old man looked toward heaven.

Suddenly the light shone brighter.

"What's happening?" Patrick shouted. "I can't see."

Beth couldn't see either. But she could hear.

The lions were whimpering. And the fourth man was singing. Beth couldn't understand the words. But somehow she knew that he was singing praises to God.

The songs made Beth feel tired. She pressed her back against the wall. Then she slid to the floor. She reached out a hand and felt Patrick next to her.

Beth fell asleep listening to the angel sing.

Patrick woke. The lion pit was still filled with light. But it was the morning sun shining.

Patrick looked around. The angel was gone. The lions where huddled together at the back of the den. They were still sleeping.

Beth was awake, whispering to Daniel.

"What happened?" Patrick asked. He yawned and stretched his arms.

"God sent His light in the form of an angel to save us," Daniel said.

Suddenly King Darius's voice came from above. "Daniel!" he called. "Has your God rescued you?"

Patrick looked up. King Darius's and Duzi's faces were smiling down at them from the grate.

Daniel stood. He said, "My God sent His angel and shut the lions' mouths. They haven't hurt me or the children."

The faces of Katav and Frava appeared.

They weren't smiling. "How can this be?" Frava asked. "The Jews live."

"They were innocent," King Darius said. "Daniel has always been a faithful adviser to me."

The king's head turned toward Katav and Frava. "That's more than can be said for you two. You are the traitors."

"Captain Anu is moving the stone," Duzi called to the cousins and Daniel. "You'll be out in a minute."

Beth stood on the path overlooking the lions' den. The animals were awake now. They were pacing and growling again.

The king was in his chariot. The little umbrella shaded his head. Another soldier was with him as his driver.

Frava and Katav were with Duzi and Captain Anu. They were walking to the stairs leading to the lions' den.

Patrick and Daniel stood near Beth.

Beth gave Daniel a brief hug. "You were so brave," she said. "I'm so glad I met you."

"And I'm glad I met you two," Daniel said. He put an arm around Patrick. "You are young prophets. I long to hear more about Jesus the Messiah."

The king called to Daniel, "Please join me in my chariot, Daniel, my friend."

Daniel turned toward the king. "As you wish," Daniel called.

Then the old man turned to the children again. "Will you be my students at the palace?" he asked them. "One day the Jews will return to Jerusalem. The prophets foretell this. We could use faithful children like you. You could help us rebuild the city."

Patrick shook his head. "We have other duties now," he said.

Beth nodded. "We need to get home," she said. "Duzi can take us."

"Farewell," Daniel said. "May God be with you." The old man got into the chariot with the king.

The soldier snapped the reins. The horses rode off.

Duzi came up from the lions' den. He put an arm around each of the cousins' shoulders. He quickly moved them away from the wall overlooking the den.

"Where are Captain Anu, Frava, and Katav?" Patrick asked.

Duzi said, "Oh, umm . . . they're feeding the lions." The scout's voice trailed off.

"Did they bring camel meat to feed them?" Beth asked.

Duzi hesitated. He seemed uncomfortable. "No, the lions eat something else," he said.

Just then the lions began to roar and growl loudly.

Duzi moved the cousins even farther away. He guided them to the wagon they came in. The horses were stamping the ground with their hooves.

"Where would you like to go?" Duzi asked the cousins.

Beth said, "Take us to the place where the dry lightning struck."

Duzi smoothed his thick beard. "The Plain of Dura?" he asked.

Beth nodded. She said, "That's where I think we need to be."

16

The Imagination Station Returns

Duzi stopped the wagon. They were far from the walls of Babylon. "I think this is the place," he said.

Beth and Patrick hopped out of the wagon. Duzi got off the driver's bench and tended to the horses.

Beth bent over and started kicking the sand. "I found another one!" she said. She held up an odd-shaped piece of glass. "We landed here."

Beth felt the yellow gadget vibrate. She turned her back to Duzi. She took the meter out of her sash. It began to flash yellow.

Suddenly the meter flashed red. A bolt of lightning shot across the sky.

A loud clap of thunder followed. The horses began to get restless. Duzi held their halters so they wouldn't run away.

"Your God is showing His power," Duzi said. "I've seen that He's a better God than Adad."

The car Imagination Station appeared.

Patrick reached for the door. "Yikes," he said. "It's even hotter than before."

A voice came from inside the machine. It was Eugene's. "Get in," Eugene said through the speakers. "Your next adventure is to find Nikola Tesla. Only he can get us all back home."

"Nike cola who?" Patrick asked.

Beth interrupted. "How are you talking to us, Eugene?" she asked.

"I got Mr. Pinkerton to give me back the computer," Eugene said. "But it has only a little battery power left."

Duzi called to Beth. "Who are you talking to?" he asked.

Beth saw Patrick get inside the Imagination Station.

"Good-bye, Duzi," she said, waving to her new friend. "It's our time to leave. Tell Daniel the Temple gets rebuilt."

Beth felt a static shock as she climbed inside the machine. The seat made her skin tingle.

Beth grabbed the knob on the dashboard. "Ouch," she said. "It's hot."

Patrick took off his coat. He put it over the knob and pulled it back.

The windshield began to spin.

"Wait," Eugene's voice said through the speakers. "I forgot to—"

Suddenly it was silent. Everything went black.

To find out the title of the next book in the series, visit TheImaginationStation.com.

Secret Word Puzzle

Many prophets in the Old Testament foretold about Jesus, the Messiah. One of them, Ezekiel, lived outside of Babylon. People from Jerusalem would come to the bank of the Chebar River to seek his advice. (That place is now called Tel Abib.)

One of Ezekiel's more famous prophecies is written in Ezekiel 34:23-24. In that verse Ezekiel gives Jesus a special name. Jesus also uses this name to describe himself in John 10:11. To find that name, use the code to fill in the sentence. The last word is the secret word.

___ ___ ___   ___ ___ ___   ___ ___ ___ ___
O   A   M   T   O   E   H   I   I   A

___ ___ ___ ___ ___ ___ ___ ___ .
S   H   E   M   H   E   R   A

= A	= H	= O	= V
= B	= I	= P	= W
= C	= J	= Q	= X
= D	= K	= R	= Y
= E	= L	= S	= Z
= F	= M	= T	
= G	= N	= U	

Go to **TheImaginationStation.com.**
Find the cover of this book.
Click on "Secret Word."
Type in the answer,
and you'll receive a prize.